About the Book

Po Threefeathers liked the old Indian ways best. He loved living with his grandmother and hearing her stories of how Paiute life used to be. She knew the important things: how to weave a waterproof bottle or make a boat out of hollow reeds. Po couldn't understand why his young uncle had chosen to study at the white man's schools. What use was white man's knowledge to an Indian? He didn't want to be an Indian with all the color washed out in school. He was content with his life as it was.

But when Grandmother was taken sick, Po found out that changes had to come. At the Indian boarding school, he met young Indians of many different tribes, with different ideas, customs, and traditions. He learned that the choice he had to make was not as simple as he had expected.

RIDE THE CROOKED WIND is an understanding and genuine story of a boy who must confront and reconcile two cultures, each valuable in its own way.

To Anne Alexander

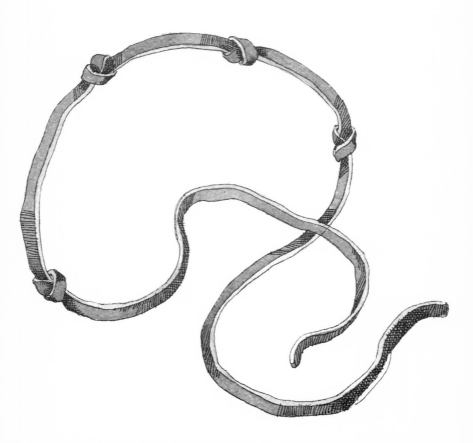

Ride
the
Crooked Wind

BY
DALE FIFE

ILLUSTRATED BY RICHARD CUFFARI

Coward, McCann & Geoghegan, Inc.   New York

ACKNOWLEDGMENTS:

To the sons of Wm. R. Palmer, author of
Why the North Star Stands Still, (Englewood Cliffs, N.J.,
Prentice-Hall, 1946), for the use of the legend
"Why the North Star Stands Still."

To Jack Freedman, London, England.

To Nellie Shaw Harnar, Pyramid Lake Indian Reservation,
Wadsworth, Nevada.
To Patricia A. Tyndall, Carson City, Nevada.

SBN: TR-698-20249-X
SBN: GB-698-30502-7

Library of Congress Catalog Card Number:
72-89766

PRINTED IN THE UNITED STATES OF AMERICA

09213

Contents

» 1 «

The Crooked Wind

Po THREEFEATHER lay on the lip of Black Wolf Rock, listening. He could hear it—his enemy, the school bus—come to a stop one hundred feet below.

He wriggled near the edge and saw the door open, kids climb on. Who'd stay back with him? he wondered. Somebody always did.

Behind him, he heard a scraping and turned his head. Two today. Billy Wilson and Chip Hawk were climbing over the edge of the western side of the rock, the only place Black Wolf could be scaled.

Billy Wilson—great. He was a steady friend, a full-blood Paiute, same as Po. But Chip Hawk? Holy Kanootch! He wasn't even all Indian.

The bus below honked twice. The door closed.

Po grinned. He reached for his slingshot and, just as the bus started up, carefully aimed at the roof right over the driver's head. Ping! On target. He wriggled back to where the boys were taking cautious peeks.

7

"YAHOO!" Chip yelled. He was a skinny kid with a narrow face. "YAHOO!" he yelled again.

"Clam up," Billy said. "You want the bus to come back?"

Po knew the bus would not turn back now. It had reached the main highway and was on its way to the big school in the next town forty miles away. The smell of its exhaust lay on the air like the trail of a skunk.

In the old days, a brave added another feather to his war bonnet when he had outwitted an enemy. Po had lost count of the times he'd missed school. Maybe enough to have a double-tailed bonnet. He reached into the pocket of his jeans and pulled out a strip of buckskin.

"What's that knotted string you're always fooling with?" Chip asked.

"A Paiute pass."

"What's it for?"

"Nothing now. Years ago when the tribes were at war if a stranger wanted to go through Paiute country, he had to have one for safe passage. They were of sinew then."

"How'd he get one?" Billy asked.

"From the chief. He tied the knots and told him what to do—wave it if a warrior stopped him on the trail. The warrior would untie a knot and let him go on again."

Billy reached out to feel the buckskin. "It was kind of like a passport, like people use now to get into other countries."

"That's right," Po said, untying a knot.

"You're not going anywhere," Chip said. "What you untying a knot for?"

"I got a day off, didn't I? I'm going to the river."

With the bus gone, Po felt free as a bird. As if he could fly across the sky so wide it dwarfed the mountains that rimmed the desert, where nothing moved for a hundred miles. Excepting that far-off crooked wind doing its devil dance. "Look away from crooked wind," his grandmother said of the whirlwinds. "Crooked wind bring bad luck. Maybe someone die." Po thought just once he'd test it. He stood out on the edge of the ledge and he did not turn away.

It was then his gaze caught the flash of a car emerging through the northern pass. He watched it. Small. Red. It looked like his young uncle's car. Holy Kanootch! It couldn't be his father's brother. Not today. The Tribal Council meeting wasn't until next week. "Hey, Billy," he said. "How do you make out that car?"

"Black wheels, ski rack on top, fast driver. It's your Uncle Lee."

"Let's beat it," Chip cried.

"You scared of him?" Billy asked.

"No," Po said quickly. Maybe too quickly. He wasn't scared of him, but he didn't like what he was trying to make of him. Po's parents were dead. As far back as he could remember he'd lived on this reservation with his mother's mother. She was one of the old ones, with the old ways. To her, his father's people, who lived on the northern reservation by the Desert Lake, were "Paiutes with the Indian washed out in the white man's school." Po didn't want to be like his young uncle.

The car was hurtling closer. Still Po stayed on the ledge until it turned into the reservation road. Then he whirled, leaped back to the hulk of Black Wolf, and led the way down its steep flanks.

It was the first time he'd cut school when his uncle was on the reservation. But he'd outwit him. That would be worth untying two knots in his Paiute pass.

» 2 «

The Pinto Pony

At the base of Black Wolf, Po picked up his school lunch bag where he'd left it. He began to run along the narrow, dusty back road. He felt the warm wind in his hair, in his throat, excitement exploding in his chest as he raced away.

Magpies flew noisily out of yellow rabbit weed growing along the edge of the road. A chipmunk scurried for cover and a lizard hurried out of the way. He passed a turkey farm and a potato field, but he didn't stop until he reached Long Pete's ranch. He darted behind one of the square haystacks standing in the field and scanned the road behind him. It was empty but for the running boys trying to catch up.

Long Pete's black hounds came rushing, snarling, but they whimpered affectionately once they sniffed his jeans. As Billy and Chip ran up, they started barking all over again.

"Holy Kanootch! You'll get us all in trouble. Quiet," Po commanded.

The boys leaned against the haystack, laughing, catching their breath.

"I thought an evil spirit was chasing you, the way you ran," Billy said.

"You mean he ran as if he was scared of his uncle," Chip said. "Know what my brother, Smoke, says? He says your uncle is going to catch up to you one day and he'll lasso and bridle you. Know what he calls him? Chief Manybooks."

"What does Smoke know about anything?" Po said. It was okay for him to hate his uncle, but not for anyone else to put him down. Especially Smoke. "Let's go," he said, starting for the river.

Long Pete's ranch was the finest on the reservation. It was along the river where the earth was rich. The barn was big and the house was shaded by cottonwoods. Long Pete allowed no fooling around his place, but he never minded Po taking a shortcut through it.

Today, as always, Po couldn't resist going by the corral to see the horses, especially the pinto. But the pony was not in the large corral. Then Po spotted him alone in a smaller enclosure close by and went over to him. At his whistle, the pony's head came up and he trotted over; Po stroked his nose. "What you doing in here all by yourself, fellow?"

Chip came alongside. "I'd sure like to ride him," he said.

"Who wouldn't?" Po asked. One day he would have just such a pony of his own. Together they would ride the wide desert and the high trails.

Chip hoisted himself up on the corral fence. "I'd like

to race him like they do in westerns—up steep canyons, across rivers, full gallop."

Po was disgusted. "If you rode a horse like that, he'd drop in his tracks."

Chip swung a leg over the fence. "No one's around. Let's. Me first . . ."

Po wanted to hit him. If the pinto were his, he wouldn't want just anyone riding him, especially Chip. "Come on," he yelled, and streaked for the river. The boys would follow him. They always did.

At the riverbank, he grasped a branch of a willow tree and swung down to the karnee, the little wickiup he had built of poles and brush in this, his secret place. Here he kept his fishing tackle and a few possessions. There was just enough room for the three of them to sit cross-legged on the pine needle floor.

It was the first time Chip had seen it. "How'd you come to make it?"

"My grandmother told me how. She lived in one when she was little."

"I'll bet it was fun and she didn't have to go to school either," Chip said.

"Not for one day," Po said. "Still, she knows more than anybody."

"So why do we have to go?" Chip asked.

Billy spoke up. "My father says you have to if you want to be somebody."

"So? Being Indian is being somebody," Po said. "What does school teach us about that?"

Still, he had sort of liked the little school on the reservation. But after the sixth grade he had to take the yellow bus to the big school where most people were strangers and he was "one of those Indians who all look alike." With the rest of them, he had sat in class with a shut-up face. Still, he had listened. The day came when no one knew the answer to a math problem, no one but he. He forgot about "staying equal," and he spoke up.

The teacher was pleased, and from that day on she called on him. She made him "stand out." His friends began to shut up their faces to him. He had to make a choice—skip school, or stay quiet and let the Anglos give all the answers. It was easier to stay away. Each time he did, one or two boys trailed him.

Now Chip offered cans of Cokes from his school-bag. Po opened one and took a sip. It was warm. "Where'd you get it?"

Chip rolled his eyes. "Fell off a truck."

Po's grandmother did not scold if Po didn't go to school. Many reservation boys didn't go beyond the sixth grade. But she would question Po's having anything that "fell off a truck." She would be quick to say: "You're Paiute. Not an Apache raider."

Po loved his grandmother. She was wise. She told him important things—about the birds that make the wind blow and about putting red paint on moccasins "because rattlesnakes don't like red." She knew how to weave a waterproof bottle and how to make a drum from raw-hide. He got to his feet. "Who's for helping me make a tule boat?"

"You going out into the marsh to get tules?" Billy asked.

"I already got them yesterday," Po said. "Cattails too."

"No one knows how really to make one of those any-more," Chip said.

"My grandmother does. She told me how."

"Is she sick?" Billy asked. "My mother said that some of the old ones were going to hold a sing for her."

"She's fine," Po said sharply.

But as he went to the edge of the river, he thought of something. The rose hips had turned red in the valley, a sign that the pine nuts were ripe in the hills. Pine nut time was a happy time. But his grandmother had not made ready to go to the harvest.

And then he remembered the crooked wind. He had not turned away from its bad luck.

He was suddenly afraid.

» 3 «

The Tule Boat

"How do you start to make a boat?" Billy asked as he followed Po to the river.

"I know how I'd start," Chip said, kicking at the big stack of tules. "I'd throw all these weeds into the river. Why not just get some boards and make a raft?"

"Because I want to know what a boat made of hollow reeds was like, that's why," Po said. "You fellows want to help? Divide the tules into two even bundles."

"You're pretty good at bossing," Chip said. "What's your job?"

"First, I've got to toughen the cattails," Po said, and he pushed them down into the river. When he thought they were well soaked, he called to Billy. "Want to help make the rope? The idea is to lap the tips of the leaves far enough to make as much rope as we want, then twist. It'll come out strong enough not to break or unwind."

"How much do you need?" Billy asked after a while, rubbing his hands on his jeans.

"Enough lengths to bind each bunch of tules at six places and to tie them together at the ends. I guess maybe we've got enough."

17

"How long will the boat be?"

"As long as the tules—about eight feet. This one is going to be big enough for just one person."

Chip, who was finished with his job and not much interested, stood on a fallen log and skimmed rocks across the river while the boys worked. After a time, he came over to see what they were doing. "Call that a boat?" he snickered as he watched them bind the tules with the cattail rope. "Looks like a bird's nest." He crossed his arms over his chest. "Big chief now see why warriors lose battles. Indian navy use straw boats."

"Oh, go jump into the river," Billy said.

It was nearing noon and they had been working all morning. "Let's eat," Po said.

"Now you're talking," Chip said.

They sat in the shade of the willow and traded sandwiches and cookies.

Po reached for a cattail root, peeled it. "It's supposed to taste like a banana," he said. He bit into it. "It does, kind of."

"A fishy one, I'll bet," Chip said. "Say, why're you always doing things like the old ones?"

"I like to know how they lived," Po said.

"I like the new ways," Chip said. "I want to move fast. I think maybe I'll be a racing car driver, or maybe a cowboy, and I'll follow the rodeos and pick up lots of prize money. My brother, Smoke, he quit high school and now he's got a job and a motorcycle. He really travels. Whoosh, and he's away."

"What does he do—what kind of work?" Po asked.

"All kinds," Chip said. "One week this, another that. He's got a great job now with a carnival at Carson. He sets up ducks in a shooting gallery and gets to ride everything free. It's like the Fourth of July every day."

"Say, what does your Uncle Lee do?" Billy asked. "He always seems important, dressed up, carrying around a briefcase."

"He's got a neat car," Chip said. "Bet it goes ninety miles an hour."

Po shrugged. "He does something about tribal relations. He travels to all the reservations in the state and even up into Oregon and Utah."

"My father says he's smart," Billy said. "I guess he had to go to school a long time to be that smart."

"I counted. Sixteen years," Po said. "He just got out a year ago."

Billy chewed on a cookie. "My father said he was on the boxing team the year the Indian school won the championship."

"Know what my father says?" Chip asked. "He says your uncle's always getting up in tribal councils giving advice: 'Your children belong in school, not in the hills harvesting pine nuts. Plant this, don't plant that.' "

"Yeah?" Po said, ramming a stick into the ground. "What does your father grow?"

"Nothing. He says it's not Indian to divide the earth into pieces, fence it, and dig into it. Well, that's true, isn't it?"

"It's the way it was in the old days," Po said.

"Besides, my father's more than twice as old as your uncle, so why should he listen to him?"

"No reason," Po said. "I don't, and I'm only half as old as he is." Po didn't want to talk anymore about his uncle. "I'm going to finish my boat," he said.

"I've had enough of those weeds," Chip said, wandering off. "See you later."

Billy followed Po and watched as he began trimming the prow and the stern. "What did they use before knives?"

"The shoulder of a deer."

"No one ever told me about things like that," Billy said.

Po sat back on his heels. "Only the old people, like my grandmother, know such things. It must have taken a long time to make a boat using the shoulder of a deer."

"Yeah," Billy said. "First you had to catch the deer."

Po stood and tramped the tules to form a deeper hollow.

"Hey, it's beginning to look like a boat," Billy said.

"Now you pull up the prow while I bind it with more cattail rope. The last thing is the gunwale."

When the boat was finished, Po lifted it up with one hand. "Light as balsa," he said. "Now we'll see if she sinks or floats."

At that moment a plane flew high overhead, trailing a long white feather in the blue sky.

"Holy Kanootch!" Po said, squinting up at the sky.

"If it's on time, it's three forty-five, time for the school bus to be coming back," Billy said. "I've got to be going. But I'd sure like to see you try out the boat."

Po wanted to get the boat into the water right away, but Billy had been a great help. "O.K., tomorrow then," he said, stashing the boat behind his brush shelter. "Say, what happened to Chip? He didn't come back."

"Who can tell about Chip?" Billy asked as they climbed the riverbank and walked toward his house.

» 4 «

Young Chief Manybooks

BILLY lived in the third house in a row of prefabs. They were of blue, yellow, and pink stucco and looked to Po like painted marshmallows on the sunbaked ground.

Billy's mother was in the yard taking down the washing. She had on a pink dress and a pink ribbon around her hair. Po wondered what it would be like to have a young mother.

"There are Cokes in the refrigerator," she told the boys, so they ran inside and got some. Then they went into Billy's room. He had his own desk and a study lamp. But soon his mother came into the room and asked if he had any homework to do.

So Po left and started home. He cut through Long Pete's ranch. All the while, he was thinking about how his grandmother never interfered with his schoolwork. She might ask him what nuts and berries were ripening along the river, or had he found any mud hen eggs, but she would not look to see if he brought home a book.

As Po neared the small corral he heard voices. Long Pete and Dave Wahe were talking together. Dave Wahe was the head of the Tribal Council. Most of the older people called him the chief.

Both men wore jeans, plaid shirts, and straw hats with wide, rolled-up brims. Wahe was a hulk of a man who seemed carved of native redrock until he smiled. Then his whole face lit up. But today he wasn't smiling. Something was wrong. For a moment Po thought to steal away. Instead, he stood where he was until Wahe caught sight of him and beckoned.

Wahe's gaze lingered on Po's face. "Were you in school today?"

"No."

Long Pete spoke up. "A nighbor saw three boys fooling around the corral this morning. Three boys who should have been in school."

"Were you one of them?" Wahe asked.

Po nodded.

"Did you ride the pinto?"

"No."

"Who stayed away from school with you *this* time?" Wahe asked.

Po looked straight at him. He didn't answer.

"Someone rode him," Wahe said. "Someone without good sense."

Po wanted to get close to the pony, but the Chief blocked his way. "You go home. Now," he said.

Bridling at Wahe's unaccustomed tone, Po started for the road. Kids stole rides on horses and it wasn't such a big thing. But the fine pinto. That was different. What had happened. Had Chip ridden him? Po had to know.

Chip's family lived in a battered trailer parked in a dry

wash. It wasn't on Po's way home, but now he was determined to see Chip.

When he reached the place, the trailer was gone. A boy came along on a bicycle and Po asked him about it.

"They've gone to the pine nuts," the boy said.

Po turned toward home. Now it was late. Well, at least he wouldn't have to see his uncle. He'd have left by now.

He came to the part of the reservation where the houses were scattered and worn. From a distance he glimpsed the only home he had ever known. It stood, half hidden, beside a cottonwood tree, as comfortable looking as the moccasins his grandmother wore.

As he neared the hut, he imagined he could smell the stew his grandmother was making from the rabbit he'd snared yesterday and the pan bread cooking.

But when he burst into the kitchen, it was empty. The black wood-burning stove was cold.

He pushed into the main room and stopped short. His young uncle was sitting at the oilcloth-covered table, writing. In the dim room, his white, open-throated shirt blazed against his smooth, coppery skin. He glanced up slowly, pushing the thick sweep of hair back from his forehead. His black eyes steadied on Po. In an instant Po knew this was not going to be like other visits and that his uncle was aware of everything.

His uncle got to his feet. "Hi, Po," he said. "I've been waiting for you."

» 5 «

The Enemy

Po's grandmother was not where she usually sat when his uncle visited—in the far corner, silent.

"Your grandmother is outside," his uncle said with a glance toward the open front door, beyond which stood a willow sunshade. "Wait, there is something I must tell you. . . ."

For a moment Po thought he saw sorrow in his uncle's eyes. And then he spoke. "Your grandmother is going into the hospital. She wouldn't leave until you came. The doctor will be back for her soon."

Po felt as if his uncle had thrust a hard fist to his jaw and his head was reeling. He rushed for the outside. His uncle moved swiftly between him and the door, blocking the way. "Listen first," he said. "Dave Wahe telephoned to me yesterday to tell me about your grandmother. I came this morning. After we talked, we drove to your school . . ."

Po glared at his uncle. He said no more about school.

"So it was up to Wahe and me to talk to the doctor, to decide what to do."

"You had no right," Po said. "You don't know my grandmother. She does not want a doctor. She's afraid of the hospital. Her old friends come here on days when she isn't feeling strong. She can cure herself. She knows all the medicine plants . . ." His voice dried up and it hurt to swallow.

His uncle put a hand out toward him. Po backed away. He was not a child.

"Her cough would not go away. It's been too long," his uncle said, letting his hand drop to his side. "The time has come when something must be done."

Po knew about coughs that would not go away. The school nurse had explained it, and just recently everyone on the reservation had had a chest X-ray. But his grandmother's beliefs and ways were different. "You're making her go, and she doesn't have to," he said, pushing past his uncle and through the door to the outside.

His grandmother was sitting in a chair under the willow shadow. She often sat just so looking across the sweep of desert and up at the cloud pictures in the wide sky. She saw signs of things to come in their shapes.

But today her eyes were closed. Her old friends, Pansy Bird and Maggie Blue, were sitting on the ground close by. Po stood before his grandmother and looked down at her. When had her firm round face, with its fringe of silver-dark hair, begun to wither like an apple? He felt scared. When she opened her eyes, he thought she must be scared too. He felt a fierce need to protect her. "I'll take care of you," he said.

She shook her head. "It is to be. It cannot be undone."

27

The words were said with such finality that Po knew it would be just so.

And now, coming far down the road, he saw the hospital car. He glanced angrily at his uncle, who had come outside. He had done this. They were helpless against him.

He moved to his grandmother's side, pressed his body against her. "The hospital is good for some things," he said, trying to make his voice sound as cheerful as a morning bird. "When Billy broke his leg, he went, and the doctor fixed it good as new. And when the eyes of old John Cornbread filled with mist, he was made to see again."

"Come where I can see your face, Poito," his grandmother said, and he crouched on the ground before her. She took his hands between hers and held them tightly, but for just a brief moment. When she spoke again it was in the gentle tones of Paviotso. "To stay free, you must hold your life in your own two hands. You will remember this?"

He nodded.

The hospital car was stopping. The doctor and a nurse got out. His grandmother stood. She brushed aside those who would help and walked, straight-backed, to the car. Once inside, she did not look back. The car pulled away. Dust circles trailed it along the road and out of sight.

Pansy Bird and Maggie Blue left silently, and then there was just his uncle.

The sun, dropping behind the Sierra, cast a purple shadow over peaks and foothills. The sage turned silver-blue. The fragrance of woodsmoke from supper fires hung in the air. It was the good and the sad time, between day and night. Po ground his teeth together to hold back the tears. But it was more than he could do. His uncle turned away and went inside. He did not "see." That much of an Indian he was.

But Po knew that he was the enemy—enemy of the life he loved. He must somehow fight against him. It would not be easy.

He wandered to his melon patch, feeling forlorn. He had planted the seeds in the face of everyone's saying melons would not grow on the sunbaked ground. But two had made it. It had meant the carrying of a lot of water and, some nights, covering the plants. They needed water now. He got a bucket from the lean-to at the back of the hut and went to the well to fill it. He remembered that his uncle liked coffee and that there was probably no fresh water in the kitchen. But he did not take water to his uncle. He poured it all on the plants.

His uncle had come outside again. He was leaning against the hut, watching him. "On the way here this morning, I passed many melon farms in the valley," he said. "Trucks were loading tons of them."

"They must have lots of water," Po said.

"Yes. Ours."

"Ours?"

"Before dams were built and the water was diverted to the ranchers. Come and eat. I found cold meat and made sandwiches."

His uncle sat at the outdoor table. Po took a sandwich,

but he did not sit. He ate leaning against a pole of the willow shadow.

"We'd better make plans," his uncle said after a while. "I can't talk to your back."

Po sat opposite him, untying the knots in his Paiute pass.

"You can't live here alone," his uncle said.

"My grandmother will be back."

"It will take a long time."

"I sometimes do chores for Long Pete. He has a bunkhouse on his ranch. I can stay there."

His uncle shook his head. "Today someone stole a ride on Long Pete's finest pony. The pinto already had a sore leg. Now it's really bad. I wouldn't count on doing any work for Long Pete."

"I didn't ride the pony," Po said, his heart sick about the pinto.

"I believe you," his uncle said. "But how about the boys who followed your lead and stayed away from school?"

"I didn't ask them to. It's not my fault."

"You know what we say: 'A man no one listens to needs no guard on his tongue. A man no one follows can go where he wants.'"

Po shoved the buckskin in his pocket. His uncle was putting the blame on him for what happened to the pinto, the pony of his heart. He would wound his uncle as much as he had been wounded. He chose his words carefully. "I am Paiute. I do not follow my white-Indian uncle's ways."

His uncle's face was still. But in his black eyes Po saw

fury. He was suddenly aware of his uncle's hands, although he had not moved them—strong, quick hands that could drop him with one stroke. Still he did not draw away.

A hot wind blew off the desert, bearing stinging grains of sand. It whipped at his uncle's hair. He did not brush it back. It fell to his eyes, making him seem more boy than man. And Po was hard pressed not to turn his eyes away. Silence lay between them, broken only by the whimpering of the wind.

When his uncle spoke again, his voice was without feeling. "You prefer the old ways, so then let us handle this problem the old-time Paiute way. Let us go back a hundred years. Imagine the situation to be the same. Your parents are dead. Your grandmother is not able to care for you. You are twelve years old. According to our way, you are a youth and then you are a man. But you are not yet that man. What is to become of you? Are you left to forage for yourself? Certainly not. You have an extended family. Your cousin is your brother. And your uncle—?"

Po stiffened. What kind of trick was this?

His uncle leaned across the table. "Your uncle becomes your father!"

Po drew back sharply.

His uncle crossed his arms over his chest. "O.K. Now you tell me what happens to that youth of a hundred years ago. Is he allowed to ride off on his pony in all directions, or is he schooled in the laws and taboos of his tribe? And what will his uncle-father do if that son will not listen?"

"It isn't *Nehmu* to change another's way. Why are you doing this to me?"

His uncle's gaze went to the melon plants. "Because you are a stubborn Paiute. And that's the kind we need. Do you know how leaders were chosen in the old days? The man most able and most daring led the antelope hunt. Only the man most skilled could head the rabbit drive. Leaders were chosen for their skills. It was a matter of survival of the tribe. It is the same today."

He got to his feet and stood in front of Po, hands on hips. "You hate me, and right now I don't like you very much. But I find myself in the unwelcome role of your father and must do something about my defiant son. I have no wife. I am away much of the time. So what am I to do?"

Before he said it, Po knew the answer: Indian boarding school.

Well, let his uncle take him to that prison. He could not make him into anything other than he was. When an Indian makes up his mind, he'd die rather than yield.

Had his uncle forgotten that?

» 6 «

The Paiute Pass

MAYBE if Po's roommate, square, stolid Dan Pioche, hadn't been too busy to show Po around this first morning, he wouldn't feel so lost.

"I'm a Washoe from the Tahoe Basin," Dan had told Po last night. "I'm supposed to herd you around tomorrow, but I'm in 4-H and I've got this sick calf, and the vet's coming first thing in the morning. But I'll tell you just what to do. Now, after breakfast. . . ."

But Po skipped breakfast. He couldn't face the cafeteria alone. He heard the scuffles in the corridor as others left. Outside his window, the trees and shrubs were so thick he couldn't see the sky or the mountains. He had once seen a mountain lion that had been caught and caged. He knew now how that animal felt. He wondered if his grandmother in her hospital room felt as trapped as he did.

When it was almost time for his first class, he left and walked down the long corridor and through the dorm door. He stopped there and looked out over the campus. He could see boys in groups, girls gathered about the school entrance, talking. He had never felt more alone. He hadn't the courage to cross over to the school building. Maybe in a minute.

He reached into his pocket and drew out his Paiute pass, the only piece of home he had. He fooled with it, untying the knots, then twirling it like a mini-lariat, whipping it around and around, faster, faster.

Suddenly, the dorm door burst open. A tall boy, about his age, rushed out. Somehow, as he did, the lariat caught his fingers. "Ouch," he yelped as the buckskin jerked tight and sprang from Po's hand.

Po grinned. Holy Kanootch, he had never caught fingers before. He grabbed at the folder that slid from the boy's hand. Missed. It tumbled down the steps. Drawings scattered onto the sidewalk.

Po was about to say he was sorry, but the boy stood before him, glaring. "What's the big idea?" the boy said, dangling the buckskin in front of Po's face.

The brashness of the boy antagonized Po. "Yeah? Look where you're going, why don't you?" he answered back.

"Pick it up." The boy pointed to his papers, the Paiute pass still in his hand.

Po looked him up and down. His hair was fringed to his eyebrows, and at the top of his skull a circle of it was cut short and stood up stiff as a curry brush. His boots were hand-tooled.

"Pick up my stuff," the boy repeated.

"Pick it up yourself," Po said, and he jerked his buckskin string from the boy's grasp.

Just then the dorm counselor came outside. The boy shuffled his papers together and went on without a backward look.

Po was mad enough to forget about being scared. He gave everyone he passed a cold, hard look. He strode across the campus with what he hoped looked like the arrogance of a young brave going into battle. But as he neared the school and started up the stairs to the second floor, he felt panic.

At the top of the stairs, a circle of boys and girls about his age blocked the way. Po paused, waiting for them to move on. The tall boy—the one he had just had trouble with—was the center of the group, the others listening to him. The boy caught Po's look, and the bold eyes steadied on him.

The rest of the group followed the boy's gaze to Po. They stepped back to let him pass—but not the boy. Not until a girl with long hair, shiny as a pony's tail, tugged at the sleeve of the boy's fringed jacket. Then he stepped aside, with a mocking laugh.

Po went on blindly until he reached the end of the hall and realized he had run out of classrooms. He turned around. The chattering group was coming his way. The girl with the pretty hair smiled.

"You're new, aren't you? What's your class?"

"English."

"Oh, same as mine. Come with me."

He felt like a stray sheep following her into a classroom and up to the teacher's desk. Behind him, the students were taking their places. He felt all eyes boring into his back.

"Miss Cloud," the girl said, "we have a new student."

Po felt surprise. Miss Cloud was Indian. He never had an Indian teacher. He handed her his entrance card. She didn't waste words. "I've been expecting you, Po Threefeather. Your uncle told me about you."

She introduced him to the class and told him where to sit. He moved down the aisle. Each step felt as if his feet were in deep marsh.

» 7 «

Stranger in His Own Land

Po's seat was the last in a row and next to a round table where five boys sat, one of them that tall boy. Just his luck to have to sit near him.

All five had the same haircut. But it was plain to Po that four were imitators. They did not have the independence of that tall one.

Miss Cloud asked a student to pass out ditto sheets. "These are questions about material we have covered up to this time. Let's see what you remember."

Po looked at his copy. It was about nouns and pronouns, and what did adverbs do. If he had ever known any of these things, he didn't know them now. When the student gathered up the papers, Po's was blank.

Miss Cloud answered a knock on the door. She came back with three non-Indians, two women and a man. "We have visitors from out of state," she announced, introducing them. "They are interested in seeing how we do things here. I would like each of you to stand and introduce yourself by name and tribe." She turned to the visitors. "We have fifty tribes in this school from several Western states."

The students stood one by one:

"John Bluestone, Mohave."

"Lily Williams, Ute."

"Benny John, Hualapai."

"Shoshoni" — "Pima" — "Washoe" — "Bannock" — "Zuni. . . ."

The girl with the shiny hair stood: "Amy Star, Papago," she said, in a voice like a soft wind rustling the tules.

It was the turn of the boys at the round table. The tall one stood: "Jim Tarlo, APACHE," he said, loud and clear. The others stood, one by one: "APACHE"— "APACHE"—"APACHE"—"APACHE."

Apache! So that was it. His grandmother's never-forgotten enemy. Kidnapper of her sister in a time long ago, even before his grandmother was born.

Suddenly the room was silent. His turn? Po looked around. Every eye was on *him*. He stood. His voice came out squeaky as a mouse: "Po Threefeather, Paiute."

Miss Cloud showed the visitors to chairs along the side of the room. "Take out your readers," she said to the class. "We'll start on page thirty-six."

She brought a book to Po. It was new to him, but as he listened to the students taking their turns, he knew he could do as well as any of them. Maybe better. When it was his turn, Miss Cloud looked at him questioningly. She was giving him a chance to pass. He stood. Just as he did so, the Apache Jim Tarlo stuck his booted foot into the aisle. Po stumbled. The visitors and the students were watching. His voice dried up in his throat, as sweat rolled down under his shirt. He sat down.

Things were no better next period in science, only

that Dan Pioche was there. Afterward, they walked to the cafeteria for lunch.

"How'd it go this morning?" Dan asked.

Po shrugged. "How's the calf?"

Dan shook his head. "I keep wondering if I did something wrong. I'm good at doing things wrong in this place."

"Is the calf yours?"

"In a way. The school gave it to me and the food is paid for by the ag department. It's up to me to take care of it, and I pay back for the food when I sell the calf and keep the profit. It's a way to earn my own money. If I do okay maybe I'll get a summer job as barn boy on the school ranch in the valley. I want to be a rancher. My father works on one."

"Why do you have to go to school? Why not just get a job on a ranch?"

"That's not good enough anymore. I have to know about new strains of cattle and scientific feeding, and I have to know about crop rotation and irrigation."

"I guess they teach you how to run a ranch like an Anglo."

Dan grinned good-naturedly. "What do you want me to do, go back to a digging stick? I'm learning his knowhow, not his ways." He shook his head again. "I sure wonder if I did something wrong. Maybe I wasn't careful enough about her feed."

"Could be she was sick when you got her," Po said.

"No one else had any trouble," Dan said miserably. "I'm supposed to go home over the next weekend for my sister's puberty rites, but I don't know if I dare leave."

"You've got over a week. Lots can happen in a week," Po said, trying to cheer him up.

They had reached the cafeteria. Inside, they lined up at a steam table, heaped their plates, and sat at one of the long boys' tables. Po was starved. The creamed tuna tasted O.K. So did the vegetables.

Amy Star went by, carrying her tray. Po watched her walk over and sit down at one of the girls' tables.

Dan gave Po a knowing look. "She's class president," he said.

Dan was soon finished with his lunch. "You can go back for more," he said. "I have to get back to the barn."

That left Po sitting alone. He wished Dan had asked him to go along.

He was still a little hungry and would have liked more bread and milk, but he didn't want to walk across the big room, so he went outside and leaned against one of the buildings and watched the students. He was a Paiute in Paiute country, surrounded by the Mohave, the Taos, the Havasupai. . . . His roommate was a Washoe, once a fierce enemy. The dorm counselor was a Sioux. It was all strange. Kind of funny when you thought about it.

Then the five Apaches strode by, taking up all of the sidewalk. Jim Tarlo glanced at Po and said something in Apache to his friends. They all stared at Po.

After they had passed, Po put his hand in his pocket. His fingers closed around the Paiute pass. How long could he take this—being a stranger in his own land?

» 8 «

Indian Culture

"Hey! It's time to get us some Indian culture."

Dan's words startled Po as much as the crack between the shoulders. He had been in a different world, listening to the school band practice for the coming Autumn Festival. He almost wished he could play something.

"What's the class like?" Po asked as they walked toward the school building.

Dan shrugged. "Mr. Shaw, the real teacher—he's an anthropologist and new here—he got sick right at the beginning, so we met him and that's all. But he's back today. You know the stuff the sub had us reading. I don't know any more than you do about it."

Po had been here almost a week now. He still wasn't used to it. But he liked Dan.

They were early for class, so they stopped outside the building, waiting for the buzzer.

Po saw Jim Tarlo and his friends approaching. Today they wore black narrow-rimmed felt hats. All alike. But Tarlo wore his with style, pulled low over one eyebrow. The silver buckle on his belt glinted in the sun.

Dan gave Po the side of his eye, then busied himself

looking at the book he carried. But Po gave Tarlo a hard stare. He returned it, his eyes narrowing to slits.

The buzzer rang.

"Let's go," Dan said, starting up the stairs.

Mr. Shaw was a blond Anglo. He stood at the chalkboard drawing sketches of early Indian homes. What did *he* know, Po wondered, about Indian ways. Nothing. Absolutely nothing his grandmother couldn't tell him.

Since Po was late coming into class and there were no regular seats left, he had been assigned one in a row of chairs against the wall. It was across the aisle and one seat back from where Jim Tarlo sat.

Mr. Shaw smiled at the class. "We've lost too much time, so let's get right with it." He pointed to the dome-shaped hut he had drawn. "Anyone care to tell me what this old-time shelter was called?"

No one volunteered.

"It's a karnee," he said.

Po was surprised that Mr. Shaw knew the ancient name. "Wickiup" was what most people said. Po paid close attention.

"Our school is in Paiute country," Mr. Shaw went on. "So we'll study the Paiute nation first."

He pointed to a map on the wall. "The bands lived here, in what is called the rain shadow, east of the Sierra Nevada Range. Storms blowing in from the Pacific were drained dry by the high, cold Sierra peaks. This dry air funneled down the eastern side, drying up the water, parching the land. Anyone know how that affected the weather?"

No one did.

"O.K., you should have got that from your reading. It meant bitter winters, blazing summers. Now, how did that affect the Paiute culture?"

Po glanced around at the closed faces of the students. He could imagine the thoughts. They were watching the smile, listening to the tone of voice, alert for the false note. It was a rugged trail ahead for the Anglo.

"Are there Paiutes in the class?" Mr. Shaw asked.

Po raised his hand.

"One. Your name?"

"Po Threefeather."

"Check me out on facts, Po. Feel free to speak out at any time."

Tarlo glanced back. Po saw that the Apache had a book open on his desk but he wasn't reading. He was doodling on a sheet of paper.

Mr. Shaw went on to outline the social organization of the Paiute. He used words Po had never heard: matrilineal, patrilineal. Holy Kanootch! He was "matrilineal"—he lived with his mother's family and his descent was through her family. He wanted to ask questions. But he couldn't quite—not yet.

He saw Tarlo glance at him again, then back at his drawing. Po could see it clearly from where he sat. Tarlo wasn't doodling. He was drawing a mean-looking face, giving it an exaggerated chin. He drew a band around the head and three mangy chicken feathers. THREE FEATHERS! Po realized the outrageous caricature was of him. He was furious.

He heard the teacher's next question: "Was the Paiute a raider?"

"No," Po said, his voice so loud it startled *him*. "The

44

Apache was the raider. He raided for loot. Never for glory. He kidnapped children. Sold them. Anything for loot."

Mr. Shaw's gaze rested calmly on Po. "Check! The Paiute was not a raider," he said. "We'll get to the Apache in due time. O.K.?"

Po blinked. This Anglo might make it.

"Now, to sum up," Mr. Shaw said. "Just for survival the Paiute had to hunt constantly for foods—roots, seeds, small animals, fish, birds. He had little time for elaborate ceremonies and dances. He fought only when his land was threatened. But then he fought fiercely. He has been called the most interesting, yet the most docile of Indians."

Po saw Tarlo take a box of crayons from his pocket. He chose a yellow one. Deliberately, slowly, he stroked the three scrawny feathers. Then he looked back at Po, his eyes taunting.

Po made a grab for the drawing, but Tarlo was too quick. He snapped the book shut on the cartoon, amost clipping one of Po's fingers.

Po didn't hear anything more that Mr. Shaw said. He looked at the boot of the Apache sprawled in the aisle. Sooner or later he'd have to clear that aisle.

After class, Dan walked down the hall and to the outside with him. "You're letting those Apaches get to you."

"Well, maybe some of it is because of how my grandmother feels about them," Po said. "But wherever I am, there they are. In a band. All talking Apache. How can you know what they're saying? But there's something else about them. . . ."

"They're Apache," Dan said.

"And I'm Paiute." Po fingered the pass in his pocket as he watched Dan take off for the barns to see how his calf was doing.

Po walked toward his lodge and started up the steps when he heard someone call him. He turned to see a husky young man coming toward him. It was Charlie Hunter, his uncle's friend. Po had met him once when his uncle brought him to the River Reservation. Charlie smiled widely and grasped Po's hand. "I happened to be close by. How are things going?"

Po grinned. "Like a war dance on red hot coals."

"They'll cool," Charlie said. "Takes time."

Po wondered how Charlie knew he was here.

And then Charlie told him. "I ran into your Uncle Lee in the coffee shop—you know, the one right off the River Reservation. I was headed this way and Lee was just coming in from the southern end of the state where he's been all week. He asked me to stop by and see you. How about a Coke? I suppose I can still find the canteen."

They walked over to the small building and went inside. Charlie got two Cokes from the Coke machine, jerked off the caps, and handed one to Po. He looked around. "Hasn't changed much."

"You came here?"

Charlie nodded. "It's where I met your uncle."

The canteen had filled up with kids. The jukebox blared, and the place began to jump. Charlie and Po finished their Cokes and went outside.

"What work detail did you draw?" Charlie asked.

"Yard," Po said. "All those leaves and stuff."

Charlie smiled. "Jobs rotate every month. Wait until you get kitchen. It was my favorite—all those extra snacks. . . ."

He took a small transistor radio from his jacket pocket. "Your uncle asked me to give you this. He said to tell you he'd be here Friday night for a meeting, and he'd see you afterward. I suppose he'll stay around for the festival next day."

After Charlie left, Po went to his lodge and to his room. He put the transistor on his dresser and stood there looking at it. His uncle had sent a scout to spy on him and to give him a present. A bribe.

But he saw now that the transistor was not new. It was his uncle's very own. Po knew, because his uncle had played it in the car on the drive to the school. He reached for the knob to turn it on.

And then he remembered that his uncle had been on the River Reservation. He must have passed right by the hospital. Yet he had not sent word of his grandmother.

He left the transistor where it was and went outside to his work.

» 9 «

The Last Arrow

DAN's calf didn't improve in the days that followed. By Thursday Dan was practically living in the barn. After supper Po went out to see for himself. He looked at the animal, and there was nothing encouraging he could say. The vet and the ag instructor came to the stall, so Po left. He watched other 4-H's at work. "Need any help?" he asked a boy currying a big roan.

"Nope. My job," the boy said. "Have to get Red in shape for the parade Saturday. Some girl in the princess contest will ride him."

Po had come too late to have any real part in the festival, but he read the posters in the halls and listened to students talking about it.

Now he wandered to the corral and climbed the fence alongside some boys who were watching a group of high school girls practicing parade riding.

The boys almost fell off the fence laughing. "They'll never make it to the reviewing stand," one said.

The girls weren't all that bad, Po thought. A couple were really good. The boys were just having a little fun.

Po didn't see Amy Star until she stopped in front of him. "I made these brownies in home ec," she said, holding up a box. "I think I put too much chocolate in them."

Po suddenly felt shy, but he took one of the cookies and was just getting enough courage to tell her she hadn't put in too much of anything when she was surrounded by students, and soon all she was holding was an empty box.

He grinned and slid down off the fence. "Not one left for you. Don't make them so good next time."

She started for the gate. "I'm due at a rehearsal for the festival. Say, how would you like to help us Papagos?"

She didn't have to ask him twice. He followed her outside of the corral just as Jim Tarlo came tearing up the path. "Hey, Amy, I've been looking for you," he shouted. "Let me show you something."

Po turned away and walked toward the barn. Why let Tarlo bother him? The Apache was an ancient enemy of the Paiute, and his grandmother never forgot it. But that was long ago. He turned back. Tarlo had opened the book he carried—the same one he'd had in Indian Culture class—and was showing Amy something. They began to laugh. Hilariously. Po knew it was at the cartoon Tarlo had drawn of him. He left and strode angrily back to his lodge.

The room he shared with Dan was halfway down a long hallway. In his anger, Po knocked over and stepped on something standing against the wall between his room and the next. He picked it up. It was an unframed painting of an old woman. "Grandmother," he said under his breath and carried it into his room and to the light of the window.

The painting was so fresh it was not completely dry, and he had damaged one side of it. The background was desert and mesa. In the foreground an old woman sat under a sunshade of reeds before a hut. It was just as his grandmother often sat before her cottage. The woman wore a head shawl and a blanket around her shoulders. But it was not his desert, his mountains, or his grandmother. They were all different, and yet the heart of it was the same.

Through the open window Po could hear the students practicing the tribal dances . . . the slow rhythm of the drums: LOUD, soft; LOUD, soft. . . . He sat on the floor next to the window and thought of home . . . his grandmother . . . friends . . . his tule boat he had not had a chance to try out . . . the pinto pony . . . all the people of his life . . . the pine nut festival . . . the bonfire . . . old men drumming . . . LOUD, soft . . . LOUD, soft . . . the feet of the dancers timed to the beat . . . heel-toe . . . LOUD, soft . . . heel-toe . . . LOUD, soft. . . .

He leaned against the windowsill and the ache he had been holding at bay since he left home grasped and mauled and tore at him until he hurt all over.

The drums . . . louder . . . louder . . . LOUDER. They were inside him, pounding, POUNDING. He couldn't bear it. He couldn't bear the sight of the picture. He picked it up, just as the sound of the drums began to fade away. He opened the door and dropped the painting where he had found it.

"Say, you," a voice rushed at him. It was Jim Tarlo, with one of his ugly friends. "So you had it." He picked up the painting. "It's ruined. What did you do to it?"

Po knew he should speak openly, but looking at the Apache's bold face, he could find no peaceful words. "I stepped on it, that's what," he said, turning back to his room.

Tarlo and his friend were on his heels . . . in his room . . . the door slammed behind them. Tarlo glanced all around until his gaze rested on the transistor. He lunged for it and smashed it into the dresser mirror. "Now we're even," he shouted.

"Not quite," Po yelled. He jerked the painting from under Tarlo's arm and crashed it down over the Apache's head.

Tarlo's friend made a rush for Po, but Tarlo shoved him aside. "He's mine," he said, taking a flying leap at Po. Po swerved and Tarlo crashed into a table. The table slammed against the wall and collapsed. A picture fell to the floor, and a lamp went smashing.

There was a loud pounding on the door.

Instantly, Tarlo and his friend rushed to the window and vaulted to the ground.

Po threw the painting after them. "Keep your trash off Paiute territory," he yelled.

He turned around. The lodge counselor stood in the doorway. He walked to the middle of the room and stood, hands on hips, surveying the wreckage, no expression on his face. His glance came to rest on Po. "Who was in this with you?"

Po tightened his lips.

There was a sudden flash of fire outside the window. Po and the counselor reached the window at the same time. The waste can, just below, was ablaze. The counselor rushed into the hall for a fire extinguisher. Students gathered. The fire bell . . . the fire truck. . . .

It was all over in minutes.

Tarlo had started the fire . . . put in the alarm. Po was sure.

The counselor stood before Po. "Well, who was it?"

Po shrugged.

"O.K., if that's the way you want it. Be in my office in half an hour. Meanwhile, you're grounded."

So, Po thought, the Apache had managed to "shoot the last arrow" after all.

» 10 «

An Indian Knows
When to Leave

It wasn't long before Dan came in. He looked around. "Raid?"

"Apache style," Po said.

"The worst kind. So?"

"I'm in stockade."

"Not bad for being new! Tarlo?"

"Who else?"

"Well, there goes the junior-high part of the festival. He's the spearhead. With him grounded, they'll fly apart."

"I didn't tell," Po said.

"If you wanted to get even, you flubbed your chance. Say, isn't it tonight your uncle's coming? We'd better do something about this mess."

It was his uncle who had gotten him into all this.

"Let him see it. I don't care," Po said. "Tell me, how's the calf?"

Dan didn't answer. He threw himself on the bed and stared at the ceiling. Without Dan's saying so, Po knew that the calf had died, and the only thing he could do for Dan was not to see the tears standing in his eyes.

After a while, Dan began to talk, and Po sat on his own bed and listened. "I might as well have got a permit to go home for all the good I did," Dan said.

"Oh, yeah, your sister's rites!" Po grabbed at a chance to change the subject. "What's the puberty celebration like with you Washoes?"

"Ceremonies, dances, food. Some of the women cook the old-time hot stone way. But there'll be chocolate cake, apple pie, and ice cream too. My sister will sure be glad she can eat. She won't have had anything but water for four days. Everyone's invited. The old people will dance in a circle all night long. The kids mostly sit around drinking Cokes and watching. But after a while the drums get to them and they dance too. The old ones tell stories."

"My grandmother's good at telling stories," Po said. "Now she's sick and all alone in the hospital. I think about her a lot. If she needs anything will she ask for it? Are they good to her? I can't help thinking she's scared. She never even had an electric light. It's bad enough for me getting used to things here, but it's worse for her."

"Is that how you came here late? Because your grandmother got sick?"

"It was my uncle's idea," Po said. "How'd you happen to come?"

"There's a good ag course here. Now I've messed it up," Dan said, turning on his side, facing the wall.

Po stood and walked to the window. He wasn't even allowed outside. He felt trapped, as if he were in a cage.

Just like that mountain lion. He remembered now that the mountain lion had clawed its way free and that was the last anyone had seen of it. The lion, Po decided, had been lucky to get away, no matter what.

The half hour was up. Now the counselor. Then his uncle.

Well, he'd make up his own mind.

He turned from the window, slipped on his jacket, and put what money he had in the pocket of his jeans alongside his knotted buckskin. He saw Dan watching and grinned at him. "If an Indian doesn't know anything else, he knows when to leave," he said.

Dan got up off the bed. "I'll go with you to the road."

They walked out of the room, down the long hall, past the office of the counselor, and to the outside. They passed the stone lodges, the houses of the teachers and the staff. The canteen was the last building. Music and laughter were coming from it.

When they reached the stone-pillared entrance, Po didn't look back. He gave a little salute to Dan and then he began to run. On and on. He was free . . . free. . . .

He heard a shout and whirled about. Dan! Po waited. Then they ran together along the road. They jumped over ditches, climbed a telephone pole. Finally, exhausted, they threw themselves on the wild grass by the roadside, laughing, catching their breath.

After a while, Po sat up. "Why did you follow me?"

"Beats me," Dan said.

"You had to have a reason."

"The calf maybe . . . or home . . . the celebration for my sister. . . ."

"Would you have left on your own?"

"I'm not like that."

"Like what?"

"Like you . . . and Tarlo."

"Me—and Tarlo?"

Dan hunched his shoulders. "There are some guys lead, others trail."

His uncle's words flashed through Po's mind: "A man no one follows . . . can go where he wants."

He got to his feet. "You go back. Come out on your own if you want to leave. But don't follow me."

He knew he was hurting Dan, his friend, but there was no other way.

Dan stood. He looked at Po for a moment, and then he strode off. When he hit the road, he stopped and looked back. "If you're headed home, you can usually pick up a ride at the Indian colony at the end of this road, where it turns into the highway. Hurry. When they start looking for you, it's the first place they'll hit."

"Thanks," Po said. "But I know a fellow who works at the carnival, brother of a friend of mine back home. He has a motorcycle. Maybe I'll try him."

"The carnival's the second place they'll look," Dan said, turning back toward the school. This time he saluted.

Po started off toward the lights of the town. He looked back. It was really dark now, but he could still make out the figure of Dan trudging back to the school. Po had remembered his uncle's words. It was because of him he had wounded his friend. He hated him more than ever, for now he felt lost and alone.

But he had no time now even to hate. In less than an hour the school authorities and his uncle would be searching for him. He had to outwit them. He began to run.

When he reached the Indian colony, he did not stop. He turned into the main highway and ran toward the town. When he passed the glaring, blaring carnival he did not even glance at it. He kept right on running. For now he knew what to do. A night bus ran the length of the state, from Reno to Las Vegas. It didn't go to the River Reservation but made a stop at the junction of two highways. It was a long hike from there to home, but he could make it. No one would think of the night bus. He didn't have a moment to spare. If he made it, he would be home while they were still searching alleys and checking out hitchhikers.

He had to stop to ask the way to the bus station and found he had another mile to go. He had already run two. He was lucky he was swift on his feet.

When he came to a skidding stop at the ticket window and put down his money, the clerk said, "You just made it. The bus is ready to pull out."

He took a seat way back and huddled away from the window.

The driver lost no time getting under way. As soon as they were out of town he turned off the lights of the bus.

Po began to breathe easily. He was safe. He moved close to the window. He looked up at the stars.

He was going home.

He would see his grandmother.

He was free.

» *11* «

Home

ALMOST everyone on the bus was asleep when it made its stop at the junction. Po was out and into the shadows as soon as the driver opened the door. Here there was a gas station and a lunch counter, but all was dark. The bus zoomed off.

It was long after midnight, clear, warm, moonlit. As he started along the road toward the reservation, Po felt as if he were already home. The closer he got to it, the faster he walked, the more excited he felt. He began to run when he came in sight of the buildings huddled darkly beneath the trees. He searched out familiar landmarks—the trading post, the tribal office, the school.

When he turned onto the rutted road that led to his grandmother's hut, dogs warned each other someone was afoot. At Old Cornbread's shack, the big shepherd rushed him. Po talked to him quietly, holding out his hand. "Holy Kanootch! I'm your friend. Remember?"

The dog licked Po's hand, then trotted beside him.

Home! Po wanted to shout for joy as he pushed open

the door. It felt empty. Lonely, without his grandmother. He wished he could light a lamp. But someone might see. The homes were sparse on this part of the reservation. Lights stood out.

He went to his cot. He was tired. But now he did not want to sleep in the hut. He pulled off blankets and carried them outside and under the willow shadow and rolled up in them.

The dog lay down beside him. He liked the nearness of the animal . . . almost needed it. But he told him to go home. "Old John might miss you," he said, patting him. "Go on, now." The dog finally did as he was told. In a moment, Po was asleep.

He awakened with the sunrise. For a second he didn't know where he was. Then he remembered. He jumped to his feet, gathered his blankets, and went into the hut. In the morning light it seemed different. Small. Cramped. Strange, without his grandmother fussing about.

He had much to do. One thing he was certain of—his uncle would come to drag him back to school. He was probably on his way now. Driving fast. Angry. Well, let him. He wouldn't find him.

He got fresh water from the well. Washed up. Then looked around for food. He ate cold cereal and canned milk. Then he packed several cans of food into his two blankets, along with his swim trunks and a few other things he might need. He slung the bundle over his back and when he reached the base of Black Wolf Rock hid it in brush.

Then he set out for the hospital, only two miles away, but he had to cross the main road. It was still very early.

He passed no one as he approached the low cottagelike building. He walked to the front door, slipped in noiselessly. No one was at the desk. A woman, her back turned, scrubbing the floor didn't look up.

Two corridors led off the entrance hall. His sneakers made no sound as he walked along the one to his right, glancing into the rooms. In the first two the beds were empty. In the next he saw a man sleeping. Across the hall a small boy was jumping up and down on his bed.

He heard footsteps and ducked into a closet filled with brooms and mops. Through a crack in the door he saw a blond nurse in white slacks and blouse. When her footsteps died away, he came out, and now he was at the end of the corridor. To the right were glass doors leading to another wing. To the left was the kitchen and the back door. He heard footsteps again, and he pushed through the glass doors, although he saw the sign NO ADMITTANCE.

He stopped at the entrance of the first room. There were two beds. The one against the wall was empty. The window bed was occupied. Grandmother! He started into the room. She was asleep. "Grandmother," he said softly.

She stirred.

He felt a hand on his arm. The blond nurse. She propelled him from the room, through the glass doors, and to the waiting room. "What are you doing here at this hour, and in the contagious ward?"

He didn't answer.

"Is there someone here you know?"

He wasn't about to tell her.

The telephone rang. She turned her head and let go his arm. He made a dash to the outside.

But now he knew where his grandmother's room was.

He went around the hospital until he came to her window. It was screened, but he could see her quite plainly. "Grandmother," he said softly.

She turned her head slowly.

"Grandmother," he said again.

She raised her head. "Poito! You, truly. No dream?"

"They wouldn't let me stay in your room. How are you, grandmother?"

"I live like cradleboard baby. You come with uncle?"

"Him?" Po spat out. "I came on my own."

His grandmother started to say something, but Po saw the white uniform in the doorway. "I'll be back—tomorrow—early."

He ducked and ran from the hospital grounds along the road to Black Wolf Rock. He climbed to the top.

He sat watching the northern pass. It was just a matter of time before he would spy his uncle's car—his uncle coming to drag him back to the school. But his uncle would not find him. It would take a total Indian to track his trail.

Students would soon be gathering below to wait for the bus. He'd see Billy, maybe even that Chip. But he wouldn't let them see him.

He spotted the small red car when it was but a speck in the distance. It was coming down the empty highway at bullet speed. As soon as he was sure, he climbed down to the base of the outcropping and retrieved his blanket pack.

The shortcut to the river was through Long Pete's farm, but he wasn't about to take that even though he ached to see the pinto, to find out how he was. A small arm of the river cut through the reservation close by. When he reached the bridge over it, he made his way down to the water. There was no path, and it was a long way around to his brush hut, but no one would see him, and he had lots of time.

The way was rough, but he knew every foot of it. Finally, he reached the place where he'd built his shelter. He couldn't see it. Holy Kanootch! It was gone. Billy? Chip? Who had destroyed it?

No, there it was. He laughed out loud. He had hidden it so well he'd almost missed it.

Everything inside was as he had left it. His fishing rod was there, his few tools. He stored his blankets and

food, took off his clothes and sneakers and got into his swim trunks. Then he went outside to see about his tule boat. All the time he was away, he'd wondered about the boat, whether it would really float. Now he'd test it. He carried it to the water's edge, then went back for his fishing rod.

He looked up at the sun to measure the time. His uncle would have talked to Dave Wahe and to others by now. He would be searching the roads and the places accessible to the river.

But he wouldn't know about the boat.

Po got into it and, using a strong limb, poled away from the shore and started upstream.

The boat was watertight. Buoyant. He was proud of it.

The sun on his skin was warm and autumn mellow. Everything was golden—the weeping birch trees, the wild grass, the cottonwoods, the hills. Over it all was the wide blue sky and the cottony clouds. A kangaroo rat stood on the bank and regarded him solemnly. A muskrat swam unhurriedly to its cabin. Po felt good. He was home.

When he reached an elbow in the river that was so thick with buckthorn and elderberry it could not be reached from the land, he poled to the shore and cached his boat in the bulrushes. He would be safe here all day.

The water was shallow and warm. He swam for a while. Then he lay in the sun to dry off. He listened to the busy life about him—the twittering of birds, the rustling of small animals in the grasses, the buzz-zzz of insects. Over all was the fragrance of sun-warmed sage and pine. He fell asleep.

When he awakened, the sun told him it was late afternoon. He was hungry. By this time his uncle would be giving up the hunt for the day. He got his fishing pole from the tule boat and in a short time had snagged a cutthroat trout, more than enough for both dinner and breakfast.

He started back, letting the current drift the boat down the river. When he was opposite his brush hut he poled to the shore. He began to pull the boat from the water. Suddenly all of his senses were alert. He tensed. Glanced all around. Everything was as he had left it.

He dropped his boat, half in and half out of the water, and approached the shelter soundlessly. When he was almost there, he saw a blanketed figure lying low in back of a clump of rabbit weed. It was the oldest Indian trick.

He stood motionless. Ready for flight.

But swift as a cougar the figure was on its feet.

It was his uncle.

» 12 «

The North Star
Stands Still

Po had never hated his uncle more than at this moment. "How could *you* track me down?"

His uncle could not mistake what he meant. But he showed nothing in his face. "I just put myself into your moccasins," he said.

"They wouldn't fit," Po spat out.

"They did once," his uncle said, letting the blanket slide from his shoulders. He had on a red shirt, jeans, and boots.

Po turned back to his boat. He pulled it from the water.

"Where did you get it?" his uncle asked, coming up behind him.

"I made it."

"I thought only the old ones remembered."

"My grandmother is one of the old ones."

His uncle examined the boat bow to stern. "You're probably the only boy who knows how to make one of these. You've done it well."

Po was warmed by the compliment. Then he tightened his lips. His uncle's words were like the flattery of the Anglo after something. Po knew what it was. Him.

"I see you caught a big trout," his uncle said. "Can you spare some?"

Po went into his brush hut and brought out an old grate he had found one day. He tossed it to a spot on the gravel midway between the shelter and the river. "If you start the fire," he said.

Then he went down to the water's edge to clean the fish. He took a long time doing it. He had a beautiful cutthroat. He couldn't refuse to share food with his uncle, but he didn't have to talk to him. When he was finished, he placed the fish on the grate, which lay alongside the brisk fire his uncle had going. It would take a while before it was down to coals and right for cooking.

His uncle was sitting on the blanket cross-legged, unwrapping a package. "I stopped by Long Pete's. His wife was making fry bread. I talked her out of some of it," he said.

So his uncle had made the rounds, probably asking anybody and everybody about him.

He went back to his brush hut again, took off his swim trunks, and got into his jeans and shirt. He was slow about it. When he thought the fire might be down to coals he came out and placed the grate on it. He sat on the gravel, on the opposite side of the fire, his arms folded over his chest. He glared at his uncle, who was smoothing two branches with his pocketknife. Finally, his uncle looked up. "Catch," he said and tossed one of the sticks to him. Po didn't catch. He let it fall alongside him.

The fish began to sizzle and hiss. The smoked fish smell made Po realize just how hungry he was. He saw his uncle pick up the stack of fry bread and count. Eight. He stuck four on his willow stick and, reaching around the fire, offered them to Po.

Much as he liked fry bread, Po did not uncross his arms.

"I'm not giving you anything," his uncle said. "I'm trading. Half your fish for half my fry bread."

Po took the bread and laid it down beside him. He had to take the trade, but he didn't have to eat it.

He watched his uncle pierce one of the flat rounds with his willow stick and hold it over the coals, just close enough to heat it and make it bubble and blister all over. Hot fry bread! Nothing smelled quite as good. He swallowed. He'd wait for the fish to be done.

But when he saw his uncle draw his round of bread from the willow stick, fold it over, and bite into it, he couldn't stand it. After all, in the old days Paiutes traded with the Washoes, their deadly enemies. Maybe even with the Apaches. He took up one of his rounds and pierced it with his willow stick and held it over the coals. When it was done, he ate it so fast it almost burned his mouth. He started a second.

He watched his uncle flip over the fish. He managed to do it at exactly the right moment, when it was crisp and brown but could be turned without breaking.

When the fish was done, Po divided it and they ate the old-time, before-forks way. He thought his uncle would be clumsy about it. He wasn't.

So far his uncle had ignored him. It was getting to Po. When would he begin to rant? Start his lecture? Finally, the meal over, Po could stand it no longer.

"Why don't you get it over with?" he asked.

"Get what over with?"

"What you came for."

"And what's that?"

"First, to find out what happened in my room. Then, to give me my orders."

"O.K. What did happen in your room? I thought that maybe I had stumbled in on the Battle of Little Bighorn."

That caught Po off guard. He almost smiled. "It all started with this Apache—"

"Apache! Why didn't you pick on a nice quiet Shoshoni, or a tame Ute?"

"I didn't pick on him. We just didn't like each other from the start. You don't know what you got me into. That school isn't like it was when you went there. Now there are almost no Paiutes. But there's everything else. They're all strangers from hundreds, maybe even a thousand, miles away. And I get there late. You wouldn't know how that feels! You wouldn't know about being jumped, either. Having to smash your way out. You're a boxer. No one tries to beat you up."

His uncle made fists with his hands and looked at them for a moment. "Maybe I'd better tell you how I got to be a boxer. . . . It was in my first year high and I couldn't stand my roommate. The feeling was mutual. We lit into one another every chance we got." He grinned. "But we had sense enough to wait until we were out in the sagebrush someplace, or behind the barns."

His uncle stopped talking, but now Po was curious. "Why did you fight?" he asked.

"Lots of reasons. I can remember only one." His lips twitched. "A pretty girl we both liked. Then one day he laid me out cold. I landed in the infirmary. Not much the worse for wear. But now we were in trouble. The head of the athletic department called us into the gym. He handed us boxing gloves. 'O.K., now, whack each other by the rules.' "

"That doesn't sound like punishment."

"No? In football season when we both wanted to be out there practicing to make the team? There we were, slugging each other. I got so I hated to hit him. And that's how later Charlie and I made the boxing team."

"Charlie Hunter?"

"The same."

"But that Paiute's your best friend."

"That's how things turn out sometimes."

"Who got the girl?" Po asked.

"He did. He married her."

"Then he won after all."

His uncle chuckled. "I wouldn't say that. I saw her just last week. I don't think she weighes a pound over two hundred."

They laughed together. It was easy, good, here by the fire.

His uncle poked at the coals. "Now, what was your problem with the Apache?"

Po hesitated, then blurted: "To start with, he's Apache. My grandmother told me the bad things that happened to her family because of the Apache. But it was more than that. Somehow we were enemies right from the first, over a silly little accident. Then he's always got his band of followers around."

His uncle raised an eyebrow. "One camp. Two chiefs. Much trouble."

"I wasn't wanting to stand out. But what would you do if someone drew a picture of you wearing a headband with three scrawny chicken feathers stuck into it? Not eagle feathers. Chicken feathers, colored yellow."

His uncle doubled his fists and punched at the air.

He did understand. It gave Po a warm feeling. He went on: "So when he smashed the transistor you gave me, I conked him over the head with a painting I happened to find in the hall and which turned out to be his."

His uncle's head came up sharply. "What's the boy's name?"

"Jim Tarlo."

"Jim Tarlo? His father is a well-known artist. The boy can't help drawing. He comes by his talent naturally. The school's art instructor says he's good. Very good. You didn't know?"

"I didn't know anything," Po said, his anger returning. "You didn't give me a chance to have a say about my life. You made my grandmother go to the hospital. They treat her like a cradleboard baby. She'll die there. You did this to her."

"Is that what she told you?"

"She didn't have to. I know."

"If she is to live, then for a while she must be treated like a cradleboard baby," his uncle said.

Po tightened his lips. Darkness shrank the earth to this

one small fire and the two of them. Po waited for his uncle to say the dreaded words: "It's time to head back."

But his uncle said nothing. He stretched himself full length on the blanket and looked up at the stars. "Happy Hunting Ground is busy tonight. Everything going someplace. Do you know our name for the sky?"

"Tu-omp-pi-av," Po said.

"When I was small, it was your father who told me about all that goes on up there on Tu-omp-pi-av."

His father! Po knew almost nothing about him. It was as if he had never been. He wanted to hear about him, but his uncle said no more. Not until Po, lying on his back and looking at the stars, asked, "What did he tell you?"

His uncle put his hands behind his head to pillow it. "Many, many things. Many, many nights. We lived by the Desert Lake and we slept outside in the summer.

"He told me that Tu-omp-pi-av was an inverted world, upside down, with its mountaintops pointed to us. He said there are trees, and rivers, there are brush and flowers, and grass. Warm weather, cold weather, day, night.

"He told me that Poot-see, the stars, sleep all day, but when the darkness begins they wake up. They are restless, just like the Indians, traveling around and around, making trails all over the sky. Some nights I would try to stay awake a long time to see which way they would go."

His uncle stopped. Po was eager to hear more.

"Did you see?"

"No, I always fell asleep trying to figure out which was which, because he said some of the stars are birds.

They go away for a long time and then come back. They have been wintering where it is warm."

"Are there animals there?" Po asked.

"All the good animals are there. Cooch, the buffalo, and Quan-ants, the eagle, and Tu-ee the deer, and Cab-i, the horse. All of them are traveling, just like the Indian, following the feed and the good weather. All but the North Star. It stands still."

"Why is that?" Po asked.

His uncle shifted his position. "On earth he was Na-gah, the mountain sheep, son of Shinob, the great god. Na-gah was surefooted, courageous, always climbing, climbing. There was one very high peak, steep and smooth, that no one had climbed. It reached up into the clouds. Na-gah was proud. He would find a way. Up and up he went. He found a crack in the mountain that led him to the highest point. He could see the entire world.

"Then he heard a great rumbling, as if the mountain were coming to pieces. He tried to start back, but the rolling rocks had closed the way.

"He could not get down. There was no room even to turn around. He thought, I must die, but I have climbed my mountain."

Po looked over at his uncle. "Did he die?"

"No. Shinob, his father, was walking over the sky and saw him. 'My son can travel and climb no more,' he said. 'Always he must stand on that little spot, for there is no place he can go. I will not let him die.' So Shinob turned him into the North Star. Every living thing can see him."

"It's sad, and yet it's not sad," Po said.

"Yes," his uncle said. "He is the only star that will always be found in the same place. Directions are set by him. Travelers look at him and find their way."

A shooting star traced a graceful arc across the sky. "That's probably Wooten-tats, the hummingbird," his uncle chuckled. "He's a busy one."

"Did you believe my father when he told the story?"

"At first. And then I began to make up my own story. To me, the North Star was like our reservation. It was always there. In the same place. Unchanged. A place to go back to. Once when we went to a big city to live, and again when I was away at school, I would get mixed up

and not know who I was anymore, or where I belonged. Then I would look at the North Star and I would know there was a place I could go home to, where I knew just who I was. That's when I first got interested in making sure it would always be there, the land that is left of all we once were free to live on. I thought about ways to do this."

"What kind of ways?"

"I thought about how it was when the white man came with his horse. He could outrun the Indian, until the Indian got the horse.

"Then, when the Indian and the white man battled, the Indian used bow and arrow. He could not compete

with the white man's rifle. So the Indian got the rifle. That evened things up, but not for long, because the white man became as numerous as the desert sands, and he did not honor the earth. So I figured if we were to keep what we still had, we would have to keep on fighting, but still with his weapons."

"What kind of weapons?" Po asked.

"His skills, his knowledge. And I felt that wouldn't make an Indian a white man, any more than using the rifle made him white. I figure Indian can't be washed out. Indian is indelible."

His uncle stopped talking. Po kept his gaze on the North Star. "The reservation in the sky is bright tonight," he said.

"It needs to be," his uncle said, "for now the white man must look to it to save himself—to find his way back."

"How can that be?"

"He must learn what we remember and he has forgotten—that he cannot take from the earth without returning something to it; that earth, water, air are partner with him and must be so treated. If he will not listen, he will not survive. It is time for the white man to trade with us again—not beads for pelts, but skill for skill."

His uncle said no more. For a while Po kept watching the stars, thinking of all his uncle had said, treasuring the good feeling in his heart, dreading the moment his uncle would say it was time to go.

Still his uncle said nothing.

After a while, Po sat up and looked across the dying coals. His uncle was rolled up in the blanket, his head resting on one arm, his eyes closed, his breathing even.

Po got up and went softly to his brush shelter and got his other blanket. As he passed his uncle, he crouched close and studied his face. Was this the way his father had looked?

And suddenly he was sad. He wished he had not called his uncle a white Indian. He wished he had asked his forgiveness.

As if his uncle had heard his thoughts, his eyes opened. *"You nee—Ye we ka. . . . Now go to sleep."*

Po went to the other side of the fire and rolled into his blanket.

» *13* «

Through the Northern Pass

WHEN Po awakened, ghostly mist hung in the trees and sat on the river. He lay quietly, not wishing to awaken his uncle, putting off the evil moment when he would say it was time to pack up and leave with him.

Po thought of last night and the story his uncle had told him of the stars. His heart had warmed toward his uncle.

But there were no stars this morning.

Last night, beside the fire, had been a kind of peace treaty. The Anglo had made many peace treaties around many fires. He had said smooth words. The Indian had believed, but the Anglo had forgotten before the fires were cold. His uncle had said smooth words last night. They had made him forget all that had gone before, what his uncle had done to him and to his grandmother. He had made him forget why he had come here—to help his grandmother.

He hoped his uncle was not a light sleeper. It would be easy to disappear into the heavy mist. Cautiously, he turned his head to look at him. Holy Kanootch! There was no one there. He jumped to his feet. Even the blanket was gone. It was as if he had dreamed it all. He peered into his brush hut. The blanket was there, folded neatly.

His uncle might be washing himself. He looked to the river. Nothing stirred.

What kind of trick was this? He'd have to act quickly not to be outwitted again. Swiftly, he hid his tule boat in brush, covered his supplies in the shelter with a layer of leaves. When he left, he took with him only his blankets slung over his shoulder.

He followed the river for a ways, then climbed up to a little-used path that would bring him to the rear of the hospital. By the time he neared it, the sun was burning off the mist. It was still early, about the same time he had gone to see his grandmother yesterday. But today he would not talk through the screen. Today he must get close to her. He had many things to say. And now he knew the plan of the hospital.

When he reached the grounds, he hid behind a shed until he saw a hospital worker come out of the rear door with a trash can. When the worker's back was turned, Po raced across the clearing and slipped into the open door. He was down the corridor and through the forbidden glass doors in seconds. He stopped to listen. He could hear no footsteps. Soundlessly, he approached his grandmother's room and stood in the doorway. She was propped up against a pillow, her face turned to the window. She was waiting for him, he knew.

He saw that the other bed was now occupied, but the patient was burrowed down under the covers, only a bush of gray hair visible. He walked softly into the room. "Grandmother," he whispered as he approached her bed.

She turned her head. At sight of him, she looked alarmed and put her hand up in a gesture to stop him. "No, no," she said.

What had they done to her that she was so frightened? He had never seen such fear on her face.

"Don't be afraid," he said. "You don't have to stay here. They can't make you. That's why I'm here. Just because my uncle made you come here, you don't have to do as he says."

Her eyes flashed. "Uncle make me do nothing."

"Then why are you here?"

Her eyes filled with tenderness—that was her way with him. For a moment she held out her hands. He took a step toward her. She shook her head and let her hands drop. "When doctor tell me I can give you 'cough that will not go away,' I come. Uncle say he take care of you. He say by time I am well, maybe school for big boys like you on reservation. No need go to away school. They give you plenty eat at away school?"

Po nodded. He swallowed against the pain in his throat.

He saw her gaze go to the door. Without turning, he knew the nurse was there. She came into the room and up to Po. "It's you again."

"Grandson," his grandmother explained.

"You may stand in the doorway, but no closer, to say good-bye," the nurse said, not unkindly.

He did as he was told. His grandmother pointed to the

other bed, smiling. The patient was now sitting up. It was Maggie Blue.

"Always her daughter tell her she should come to hospital. So when I come, she come," his grandmother said.

The nurse was waiting for him to go.

"*Oo-nooz mia*," his grandmother said.

He could not answer her good-bye. He bit his lip, gave a quick wave, and ran from the room, brushing at his eyes.

He started home, his gaze on the rutted road, his fingers grasping the knotted string in his pocket.

As soon as he pushed open the door to the hut, he smelled the coffee. So his uncle was waiting. Well, he would not run again. He set his jaw and walked into the kitchen. It was empty. On the stove next to the coffeepot stood the coffee can. Propped up against it was a note: "You're out of coffee," it read. Clipped to the note was a ten-dollar bill.

Po felt the coffeepot. It was still warm. He ran out of the hut and raced up to the top of Black Wolf. Far away, a small car headed north, fast, was just entering the pass. "Uncle Lee! Uncle Lee!" he shouted.

And then the car vanished and there were only miles and miles of empty highway.

He felt empty too. He sat on the narrow shelf of rock and looked at his hands. His life was in them. His uncle had set him free. He could do as he wanted—live the life he knew—fish, hunt, visit his grandmother.

He thought of her in the hospital, and now he remembered every detail of the room—the whiteness of it, the airiness, the shining floors, the flowered curtains at the window, the TV suspended from the ceiling, his grandmother smiling, pointing to Maggie Blue. He remembered what his Uncle Lee had said: "If she is to be well again, she must be treated like a cradleboard baby."

He got to his feet, walked down the steep incline and across the dusty land to the hut. He leaned against a pole of the willow shadow. It sagged against his weight. Soon it would fall. And so would the hut.

He looked over at his melon plants, and he saw that the ground around them was dark. They had been watered. Uncle Lee. Water carried from a well. He remembered the tons of melons his uncle had told him about grown on ranches that had water. "Ours!"

Po looked far across the land. He imagined melon plants and growing things reaching to the mountains. The image vanished, and there were only the two struggling plants and the dry desert. He felt a quick anger, and he reached down to tear the plants from the ground. But his hand could not. They were living things.

He went into the house. He'd eaten no breakfast, but still he wasn't hungry. He poured himself a cup of the coffee his uncle had made. It was a strong brew. That uncle! He made a face over it, but he swallowed it. Then he threw the rest out and washed the pot.

He put the ten-dollar bill into his pocket, alongside his knotted string, and went outside, closed the door behind him. He started walking. First, he'd see the pinto.

The pony was in the large corral, frisky, kicking up his heels. "You're O.K. again," Po said, when the pinto trotted over and nuzzled him. He felt the smooth warmth of the pony's coat next to his cheek. How he wished he were his. He had been building a dream. Wishing would not make it come true.

He started walking. Now he saw things he had not noticed before—the narrowness of the strip of green along the river where the few good ranches were—the wide miles of wasteland where there was no water.

He came to the main road, and to the trading post. It was closed. A sign on the door read: "Gone up north for the Autumn Festival."

Today was the day.

When he came to the shabby tribal office, Dave Wahe's pickup was parked in front. His wife sat in the cab with the baby. She smiled and asked about his grandmother. The four older Wahe children were in the back, along with the grandparents. Dave came out of the office carrying a box. "Hi, Po," he said. He did not ask any questions.

Po gave him a hand loading the pickup.

"We're going to the Festival at the Indian school," Daisy, the eldest Wahe child, said. "You going?"

Po shrugged.

"If you are, better come with us," Dave Wahe said. "We're about the last to leave."

"Thanks, but I'm heading into the hills to harvest pine nuts," Po said, turning away and walking toward the gas station. He was sure he'd catch a ride to the mountains.

When he passed the park, where he had often played, he stopped for a moment to look at it. For the first time he noticed it was small, dusty, worn out. A few old men, as worn out as the park, were playing the hand game—passing a stick hand to hand, hiding it, wagering who had it.

When he came to the gas station, a group of older boys, one of whom he first thought was Smoke but wasn't, were goofing off, drinking out of cans, tossing the empties along the road. He had seen boys like this all his life, boys who seemed to have nothing to do but toss around beer cans. One of them motioned to Po to join them around their ramshackle car. He could go with them—be one of them.

Suddenly, he whirled and ran back toward the tribal office. The pickup was just leaving the curb. He yelled. The children yelled. Dave stopped. Po swung aboard.

While the children and the old folks chattered about the fun ahead, Po sat silent. He was riding north, but that did not mean he was going back to the school.

» 14 «

The Indelible Indians

"WE'LL miss the start of the parade," Daisy Wahe shouted to her father as they turned off the main highway and found the road leading to the school choked with cars.

"Don't worry," Dave Wahe said. "I never knew a parade to start on time."

When they reached the school, because of the crowd, they had to park outside the stone pillars. Everyone was excited now. Except Po. He felt dread.

"I hear drums," one of the children cried, and the four of them jumped from the pickup and ran, with the grandparents and Mrs. Wahe with the baby close behind.

Po sat there looking at the stone pillars. He had felt free when he escaped them. He couldn't go back through them, not even to see the festival.

Dave Wahe came around to the back of the pickup. "How about giving me a hand, Po? This is as close as I can get to the auditorium, where the women are waiting for our handicrafts. It will save me a second trip."

Po looked at the broad, kind face of Wahe, and the understanding he saw there made him choke up. He looked away and shook his head.

"When I came here," he heard Wahe say, "we didn't have cars and pickups like now to go back and forth. It was my first time away from home. I had to stay for a year. I didn't know one word of English."

"Did they whip you? Did they tie your feet together so you wouldn't run away? I heard they did."

"No," Wahe said. "They didn't do that. But we didn't have festivals like this one today, and our families weren't welcome like now. I understand they're here from all over the West."

A group of people wearing tribal costume hurried through the pillars.

"Indian dress and language were discouraged," he said.

"How old were you when you came?" Po asked.

"Six," Wahe said, taking hold of one of the boxes and hoisting it to his shoulder.

Six!

Po watched him go. He was wise. He was a real chief.

Po slid from the truck bed, picked up a box, and followed him.

When they delivered the boxes to the table marked RIVER RESERVATION, the auditorium was almost deserted because the parade was starting. Only a few women were still at the tables arranging pottery, silver, turquoise, and leatherwork.

When Dave Wahe left to join his family, Po stayed back. He wasn't ready to join the crowd. Maybe he'd never be.

He could hear the drums—closer—CLOSER—CLOSER—they were exploding inside him—pulling at him—until, finally, he ran outside to all of the color—red—yellow—blue—orange. People were lined four deep along the parade route, most in native dress or wearing some token of their tribe.

The grand marshal, in full war bonnet, astride a palomino, was just coming into view. Po hardly recognized the heroic figure as one of the ag instructors.

Behind him came the girls vying to be princess. Po had watched them practicing riding in the corral, girls in jeans and sweatshirts. But today, dressed in beaded buckskin, their mounts led by colorful braves, they looked like the pictures he had seen of Indian maidens of long ago.

There was a break in the parade. "Hey, Po," someone yelled from across the street. It was Dan. He came over, a wide smile on his face. "You're back!"

"I got a free ride up. Thought I'd see what was going on."

"Jim Tarlo's been looking for you," Dan said.

"With his gang, no doubt, to finish the fight."

"No. Alone. I told him you got busted because you didn't tell on him."

The parade was starting up again. "That's my family over there—everyone. Want to come meet them?"

"Not now," Po said, and he watched Dan run back across the road.

All the students seemed to be surrounded by family. Only he was alone. He moved on, searching the faces in the crowd, listening to the beat of the drums, and standing on tiptoe to see the floats of the tribes—the Pimas, the Hopis, the Hualapai.

He heard a great burst of applause and much laughter. Something really great must be coming up. He was in front of the school building now and he stood up on the steps to see what it might be.

The Apaches!

They were doing their devil dance, their drummers coming up behind them. They wore only deerskin over their painted bodies, black hoods over their faces, and tall, wild headdresses.

"There is something about an Apache," said an old man standing alongside Po.

"Yeah! He's mean," Po said.

Running among the Apache dancers was the clown, his body painted with white dots. He whirled and gyrated and stopped to threaten little children with his wand or to tease the pretty girls lining the curb. The tall clown was the hit of the group. Everyone applauded, pointed to him. Po, watching, knew the masked figure had to be just one person—Tarlo.

"They were the last tribe 'to come in,' " the old man said. "They put up a big fight to stay off the reservation . . . kept all the 'Bluecoats' on the run. . . ."

Po felt resentful toward the man for his praise of his enemy. He felt resentful, too, of the applause they were getting.

"They've still got some of the spirit and color of the old days," the old man said. "I envy them."

Envy them? "Not me," Po said, going down the steps. Why was he so loud about it? Was he trying to convince himself?

He felt out of all of it. Alone.

And then he saw his uncle. He was standing on the curb, close to the corner where the parade made a turn. A feeling of joy warmed Po, and he burrowed through the crowd.

As he came up behind him, he saw that his uncle was still wearing the jeans and red shirt. But over the shirt he wore an elkskin vest. A two-foot-high eagle was beaded into the back of it. That uncle! Always the unexpected. When Po crowded in beside him, he did not as much as turn his head and acknowledge his presence.

The Papago float was coming up—a desert scene—a native home, behind which sat three girls, one of them in a white-fringed dress, her long black hair in two braids. Amy Star. She waved when she saw him, and her smile was friendly and happy and lasted as long as his, which was until the float turned the corner.

When Po turned back, his uncle was giving him a sideways look, one eyebrow raised, the hint of a smile on his lips.

Po grinned, and his uncle turned back to the parade.

They watched the Shoshoni and the Washoe, the Ute and the Havasupai—all the tribes of the school. They watched the visiting tribes: the dancing Nez Perce, the Nisqually, and the Muckleshoot. And Po thought, They're Indian—indelible Indian. And the most indelible of all was his uncle-father.

When it was over, they walked together toward the field where the parade would end.

"Let me show you something I saw earlier," his uncle said, pointing to a long, narrow poster at the entrance to the field. It was a series of drawings, humorous carica-

tures of the various tribes. The poster was signed
JIM TARLO.

Right in the center was the sketch Po had seen Tarlo
make of him. But it was changed. There were no chicken
feathers. In their place was a lone eagle feather, bent
forward in the proper way, like the hand of Tobats, the
elder god. Tarlo had added something else. With the
fingers of his right hand Po was holding up the Paiute
pass. But in his left hand he wielded a tomahawk. Over
it was the caption: A PAIUTE WELCOME.

Po grinned. He got the message. That Apache. Would
anyone ever match him?

Po pulled the knotted string from his pocket. "How'd
he know what it was?"

"That's part of being an artist, knowing such things,"
his uncle said.

The Apaches entered the field, still doing their dance.
Po watched the clown weave through the crowd.
"TARLO!" he shouted.

The Apache glanced his way.

"Catch!" Po yelled and he tossed the Paiute pass
across the clearing.

Tarlo caught it, eyes gleaming behind his mask. He
whirled it aloft as he circled the crowd one more time.

Po's heart felt good as he walked with his uncle-father
to where, against the background of the snow-rimmed
Sierra, the tribes were uniting.

Po had never followed anyone. But he knew he would
walk beside his uncle-father. He would try to give him
the time he asked for—a year at a time. At the end of the
year, he was sure his grandmother would be well enough

to come to the Festival, and he'd have something to show for the Paiutes. He'd give that Tarlo some competition.

A year was long. How often would a crooked wind whirl across his path? No matter, he'd have to ride it—ride the crooked wind. It was, in the end, just so much sand.

The intertribal circle was forming. The old men were drumming: LOUD, soft; LOUD, soft; LOUD, soft.

About the Author

DALE FIFE is probably best known for her books about Lincoln Farnum: *Who's in Charge of Lincoln?*, *What's New Lincoln?* and *What's the Prize, Lincoln?* She is the author of many other books for children, including such favorite titles as *Adam's ABC* and *Joe and the Talking Christmas Tree*.

Dale Fife lives in San Mateo, California. She traveled to an Indian reservation in Nevada to do research for RIDE THE CROOKED WIND.

About the Artist

Painter and illustrator RICHARD CUFFARI has received awards from the American Society of Graphic Arts and the Society of Illustrators. He has illustrated more than fifty books for children. He does careful research into the background of each story to make his pictures authentic in every detail.

Richard Cuffari studied at Pratt Institute. He and his wife, Phyllis, and their four children live in Brooklyn, New York.